Ingenious Jean

Written by
Susan Chandler

Illustrated by
Kate Leake

meadowside
CHILDREN'S BOOKS

I can't begin to tell you just how ingenious,

Ingenious Jean was.

Or maybe **I** can?

Maybe **I** can tell you that,
while her brother and sister
were watching cartoons,
she was inventing...

something amazing!

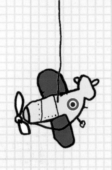

Ingenious Jean was searching in her toy box to find some good things to invent with.

She was **hammering** and **banging**,

drawing and planning,
scheming and dreaming,

until her invention was ready.
She took it in to show
her brother and sister.

'Look what **I**'ve invented!' said Ingenious Jean.

'What is it?' asked her brother.

'It's a contraption that lets one person talk to another! Even when they are in different houses!'

They all thought for a moment.

'Well that sounds ingenious!'
her brother said, picking up the phone
to call his friend.
'But I'm sure it's been done before.'

'That doesn't matter,' said Ingenious Jean.
'Because **I** have another
inventing idea!'

And with that she went back into her room to find some good things to invent with. This time, Ingenious Jean delved deep into the wardrobe.

While her brother and sister were dressing up, Ingenious Jean was inventing something **stupendous!**

She was hammering
and **banging**,

drawing and planning,
scheming and **dreaming**,

until, at long last,
the invention was ready.
She took it in to show
her brother and sister.

'Look what I've invented,'
said Ingenious Jean, once again.

'What is it?' asked her sister, through
the dress she was pulling over her head.

'It is a special box that lets you
watch moving pictures with sound!
Look what happens when
I switch it on!'

They all thought for a moment.

'It does sound ingenious,'
said her sister, turning on the telly.
'But I'm sure it's been done before.'

'That doesn't matter,'
laughed Ingenious Jean,
'because I have another
inventing idea!'

And with that, she went back into her room to find some good things to invent with.

This time, Ingenious Jean rummaged far under the bed. While her brother and sister were playing in the sandpit,

Ingenious Jean was inventing something incredible!

She was hammering and **banging,** drawing and planning,

scheming and dreaming, building and making,

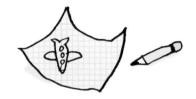

until, at long last, the invention was ready.

She took it out to show her brother and sister.

'**Look what I've invented,**' said Ingenious Jean, feeling very tired.

'What is it?' asked her brother with a bucket on his head.

'It's a vehicle that will carry people off into the sky, land in a hot country and then bring them back again after a lovely holiday.'

They all thought for a moment.

'That does sound ingenious,'
yawned her brother, as he watched
a plane leave a trail in the sky.
'But I'm sure it's been done before.'

By now, she had run out
of inventing ideas.
There was no point in going
back into her room to find some
good things to invent with.

There was no point in
hammering and banging,
drawing and planning,
scheming and dreaming,
building and making.

So Ingenious Jean decided
to forget about inventing
marvellous things and
wandered into the kitchen
to find something to eat.

She found a big bowl and poured some cold custard into it.

On top, she scooped some green gooseberry jam.

On that, she added a splodge of thick chocolate spread.

Then on went some lemon curd and the next layer was a dollop of tomato sauce.

Then, to make it **more** amazing, she added some salad cream!

To make it **MORE** stupendous, she added some peanut butter with extra crunch!

And, to make it **MORE** incredible, she added some blueberry jelly!

And then, finally, for good luck...

a pinch of salt.

The bowl had become so full
with delicious mixture that it started
to spill over the top and down the sides.

But Ingenious Jean carefully carried
it out to show her brother and sister.

'Look what I've made!'
said Ingenious Jean.

Her sister dipped her spade into the bowl
and tried some of the mixture.
Her brother scooped his bucket into the bowl
and tried some of the mixture.

'It's never been done before!'
announced her sister.

'This is the tastiest
pudding ever!'
exclaimed her brother.

They both thought for a moment.

'Ingenious Jean!'
they said at once…

...'What a marvellous invention!'

For Robert McBain
S.C.

For my baby cousin 'Leon',
who loves his bedtime stories!
K.L.

First published in 2005
by Meadowside Children's Books
185 Fleet Street
London EC4A 2HS

Text © Susan Chandler 2005
Illustrations © Kate Leake 2005
The rights of Susan Chandler and Kate Leake
to be identified as the author and illustrator
have been asserted by them in accordance with
the Copyright, Designs and Patents Act, 1988

A CIP catalogue record for this book
is available from the British Library
10 9 8 7 6 5 4 3 2 1
Printed in China